Secret PRINCESSES

Ballet Dream

ROSIE BANKS

Wishing Star Palace

The Secret Princess Promise

"I promise that I will be kind and brave,

Using my magic to help and save,

Granting wishes and doing my best,

To make people smile and bring happiness."

Story One

CHAPTER ONE
Christmas in California

"Found it!" called Charlotte Williams, trying to tug a large plastic box out from where it was wedged between a bag of golf clubs, two surf boards and a tent.

"Let me give you a hand," said Charlotte's dad, helping her drag the box of Christmas decorations out. Mopping his brow, he gazed around their garage, which was jam-packed

with sports equipment, gardening tools and beach toys. "I have no idea how we've managed to collect so much stuff so quickly!" he said.

Charlotte's family hadn't lived in California for very long, but they loved it – especially the hot weather. When they weren't at work or at school, they were usually outdoors having fun in the sun.

Charlotte and her dad carried the box into the front garden, where her mum was watering the plants and her twin brothers, Liam and Harvey, were playing catch.

"Who wants to help put up the Christmas lights?" called Charlotte, tucking her brown curls behind her ears.

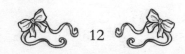

Charlotte and her dad wound a string of fairy lights around a palm tree.

"Look!" cried Liam. He pulled out a light-up reindeer. "I found Rudolph!"

Harvey held up a snowman decoration. "And here's Frosty the Snowman!"

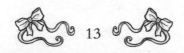

"Hey, what do snowmen eat for breakfast?" Charlotte asked the twins. Without waiting for them to reply, she said, "Frosted flakes!"

The boys chuckled as Charlotte helped them find perfect spots on the lawn for the decorations. It felt weird to be putting out Christmas decorations wearing flip-flops and shorts! Back in England, where they had lived before, it was always cold at Christmastime.

"I might barbecue a turkey for our Christmas dinner this year," said Dad, wrapping lights around an orange tree's branches.

"Yum!" said Harvey, rubbing his tummy.

"Someone at work gave me a recipe for Christmas pudding-flavoured ice cream," said Charlotte's mum. "That would be a cool

Christmas dessert."

"I'll help you make it," offered Charlotte.

"Hey! Don't forget Santa," called Liam, waving around a light-up Santa Claus.

Charlotte positioned Santa by the reindeer decoration. "There," she said. "Now he's ready to deliver presents."

Liam and Harvey burst into song:

"Surfin' Santa comes riding across the sea,

With a sack full of gifts for you and me!"

As the boys sang, they held their arms out and pretended to be surfing.

"What's that you're singing?" Dad asked.

"It's the song our class is singing in the school Christmas show," explained Harvey.

"Sing it again," said Mum, taking out her mobile phone. "I'll film you and send the video to Nana and Grandad."

Liam and Harvey clowned around on the lawn, singing the song at the top of their lungs. When they were done, Mum pointed the phone at Charlotte.

"Merry Christmas!" Charlotte called, running across the lawn and doing a backflip.

"They're going to love this," said Mum as she emailed Charlotte's grandparents the video.

"Can you send it to Mia's mum too?" Charlotte asked.

"Of course," said Mum.

Mia was Charlotte's best friend, who lived in England. Charlotte loved celebrating Christmas in California, but she missed the traditions that she and Mia had shared. They had always gone to a pantomime together, shouting out "Behind you!" and trying to catch the sweeties that the actors threw into the audience. Thinking about Mia reminded Charlotte of another friend of theirs.

"Hey, Mum," said Charlotte. "Have you seen the video for Alice's new Christmas song? It's called *Christmas Dream*."

"No," said Mum. "Let's watch it now."

Charlotte's mother found the video and pressed play. On the phone's screen, a pop star with cool red streaks in her strawberry-blonde hair danced around in a glittery silver mini dress. Twirling under falling snowflakes, she

sang about her Christmas dream coming true.

"Wow," said Charlotte's mum. "I can't believe that she used to babysit for you."

Alice had been their neighbour back in England,

until she'd won a TV talent competition
and become a pop star. But Charlotte knew
something about Alice that even her biggest
fans didn't know – she was a Secret Princess
who could grant people's wishes using magic!
Thanks to Alice, Charlotte and Mia still got
to see each other at a magical place called
Wishing Star Palace, where they were training
to become Secret
Princesses like her!

Charlotte
suddenly longed
to see her best
friend. She looked
at her special wish
necklace and bit her

lip to stop herself from shouting with joy. The
necklace was glowing!

"I'm going inside to get a drink of water,"
Charlotte called out.

She hurried indoors and pulled out the pretty
gold necklace Alice had given her. Holding
the half-heart shaped pendant in her hand,
Charlotte said, "I wish I could see Mia!"

The light from the pendant encircled
Charlotte in its glow. She squeezed her eyes
shut and let the magic sweep her away.

When Charlotte opened her eyes, she
gasped out loud. A magnificent palace with
flags fluttering from its four turrets rose up
impressively in front of her. But even more
excitingly, sparkling white snow covered the

grounds and icicles hung from the palace's heart-shaped windows!

"Snow!" Charlotte cried, spinning around. She was now magically wearing her pink princess dress, and the flowery skirt swirled out as she spun. She kicked the snow in delight, catching a glimpse of the glittering ruby slippers on her feet.

The snow showered a blonde girl in a tiara who had suddenly appeared right in front of her. She had a necklace with a pretty half-heart pendant on it, just like Charlotte's.

"Oops!" said Charlotte, brushing snow off

the girl's gold dress. "Sorry, Mia!"

"Don't worry," said Mia, giggling. She hugged her friend. "My mum just showed me a video of you and the twins."

"Did you like our Christmas decorations?" Charlotte asked her.

"Yes," said Mia. "It was funny to see a snowman next to a palm tree!"

"Tell me about it!" said Charlotte. She shivered and rubbed her arms. "Brrr! I'm not used to the cold any more."

"Let's go inside and warm up," said Mia, putting an arm around her friend's shoulder.

As they headed towards the palace, something flying through the air caught Charlotte's eye. "Oh my gosh!" she gasped.

"Is that Santa?"

"I don't think so," said Mia, squinting up at the sky.

A sleigh landed on the snow in front of the palace. Sitting inside it were two ladies wearing beautiful feathered masks. "Hello, girls!" one of them called. "Merry Christmas!"

CHAPTER TWO
The Northern Lights

"Er, hello?" said Charlotte uncertainly as she looked at the masked princesses in the sleigh.

"Sorry! I forgot I had this on," said the person holding the reins. She pulled off her mask and Charlotte saw the smiling face of Princess Ella.

"Hi, Ella!" Mia and Charlotte said together.

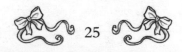

Then the other person in the sleigh took off her mask. "Surprise!"

"Alice!" Mia and Charlotte exclaimed, running over to the sleigh to greet their old friend.

"You girls must be freezing," Alice said. She waved her wand and suddenly their ruby slippers became warm boots. Both girls now had furry coats over their dresses and their tiaras had been replaced by woolly hats with big fluffy pom-poms.

"Thanks," said Charlotte. "That's much better."

"Can we pat the reindeer?" Mia asked shyly.

"Of course," said Ella, who was a vet back in the real world. "They're very tame."

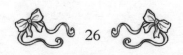

Mia gently stroked a reindeer's velvety nose and it made a snuffling noise. "What's this one's name?"

"She's Noelle," said Ella. "And the other one is called Joy."

Charlotte patted Joy's fluffy neck.

"Would you girls like to come for a ride with us?" said Alice.

"In the sleigh?" Mia asked, her blue eyes wide. "Yes please!"

"Hop in," Ella said, laughing. "There's plenty of room."

Charlotte and Mia clambered into the sleigh and snuggled under a warm blanket. Ella twitched the reins and the reindeer leaped up into the air!

"How amazing is this?"
shouted Charlotte over the wind
that made her brown curls fly out
behind her.

Mia squeezed her friend's hand
tight in reply.

The girls leaned out over the
side of the sleigh and saw
Wishing Star Palace below.

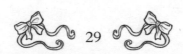

Although it was starting to get dark outside, none of the palace's lights were on. "Aren't any of the other princesses here?" Charlotte asked Alice.

"We've asked them to stay away until Christmas Eve," Alice explained, a mischievous look on her face. "Because we're planning a surprise!"

"We've decided to start an ancient Secret Princess tradition again," Ella told them, holding up her feathered mask. "In the olden days the princesses always held a masked ball to celebrate the appearance of the Northern Lights in the skies above Wishing Star Palace."

"It was one of the most magical nights of the year," said Ella. "There were beautiful lights, music and dancing."

"It sounds really fun," said Charlotte, who loved to dance.

"I hope so," said Alice. "We're going to decorate the palace so it's really special for our friends."

"That's so thoughtful," said Mia. "I bet they'll love it."

"Hopefully you will too," said Alice. "You're invited as well!"

"Yay!" cheered Charlotte. She'd never been to a ball before!

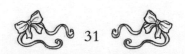

Princess Ella moved the reins again and the reindeer started to descend.

"The Enchanted Lake is the best place to see the Northern Lights," said Ella.

"What are the Northern Lights?" Charlotte asked, as the reindeer landed smoothly by a frozen lake.

"Just wait and see," said Alice, pointing up at the dark, cloudless sky.

Suddenly, a streak of glowing green light danced across the sky. It slowly changed to radiant whorls of purple and pink, the colours swirling and twirling together.

"That's so beautiful!" said Charlotte. Even though she was bundled up, her arms had goosebumps.

"Is it magic?" asked Mia, mesmerised by the changing lights.

"No," said Ella, shaking her head. "It happens when solar wind particles collide with air molecules and their energy is turned into light."

"But long ago, the Secret Princesses believed it was magic," said Alice.

"Just because we understand the scientific explanation now doesn't mean we shouldn't have a party to celebrate," said Ella. "Right?"

"Right!" agreed Mia.

As they watched the Northern Lights, a tall princess in an elegant dark green ballgown and a green mask appeared by the edge of the Enchanted Lake. A cloak with a fur-lined hood covered her hair.

"Oh, hello," said Alice. "You're early! We weren't expecting guests until Christmas Eve."

"Come and watch the Northern Lights with us," said Ella, beckoning the princess over. "They're spectacular."

Charlotte suddenly noticed a blue glow. It wasn't coming from the Northern Lights – it

was coming from her
sapphire ring, which
warned when danger
was near. But before she
could raise the alarm,
the princess in green
swept off her hood,
shaking out a mane of
long black hair with
an ice-blonde streak.
She removed her mask,
revealing cold green
eyes. It was Princess
Poison!

"What are you doing
here?" Ella demanded.

"A little birdie told me you were planning a ball," said Princess Poison, her mouth twisting into a cruel smirk.

"You're not invited," said Alice. "You're banned from Wishing Star Palace!"

"Ah, but I'm not at the palace, am I?" said Princess Poison. Princess Poison had once been a Secret Princess, but she had been kicked out for using wishes for herself rather than helping others. Now, she despised the Secret Princesses and spoiled wishes to make herself more powerful.

There could be only one reason she was here: to cause trouble!

Princess Poison whipped out her wand and hissed a spell:

**"You banished me, which wasn't nice,
So now I'll turn you into ice!
Wishing Star Palace will be frozen too,
So cold it will turn your lips to blue.
To break the spell there's only one way:
Grant two wishes before Christmas Day!"**

Green light shot out of the wand, hitting Ella first and then Alice.

"No!" yelled Charlotte. She threw her arms around Alice but the princess was frozen solid.

Princess Ella was frozen
too, just like a statue.

"You won't get away
with this!" Charlotte
yelled at Princess Poison.
"We'll break the spell!"

"Really?" said Princess
Poison, arching her
eyebrow. "But how? Ella
and Alice told all the
other Secret Princesses to

stay away until Christmas
Eve. So there's no one
here to help you."

Princess Poison climbed
into the sleigh.

"Don't let her get
away!" cried Mia.

Charlotte sprinted
towards the sleigh, but
Princess Poison quickly
slapped the reins and
the reindeer soared into
the air.

"Sorry! I've got to fly!" Princess Poison called, her cackle echoing in the cold air as she disappeared into the Northern Lights.

Then Mia and Charlotte were all alone, in the cold, cold night.

CHAPTER THREE
Double Wish

"What are we going to do?" Mia asked, staring up at the sky despairingly.

"We're going to grant two wishes before Christmas and break Princess Poison's spell," said Charlotte firmly.

"How?" said Mia.

"We'll use our ruby slippers to travel back to the Mirror Room," said Charlotte. Then she

remembered – they were wearing boots, not their magical ruby slippers!

Mia shivered. "We'd better start walking, or we'll be frozen solid too." She trudged through the snow, away from the lake.

"I thought the palace was in that direction," said Charlotte, pointing the other way.

Looking across the lake, she noticed something reflected in the ice. At first she thought it was the Northern Lights, but then she realised it was something else … it was two faces!

"Look, Mia!" she cried, running to the edge of the lake.

"It's two girls!" Mia said, staring at the ice. The girls reflected in the ice both wore black leotards. One had curly black hair and the had very fair hair and pink glasses.

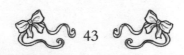

They both had their hair tied in buns.

"Do you suppose the lake is like the Magic Mirror?" wondered Charlotte.

At Wishing Star Palace there was a special room with a magic mirror. Normally, Mia and Charlotte used the mirror to find out whose wish they needed to grant.

"It might be," said Mia, crouching down to touch the ice. As soon as her fingers made contact with the cold, slippery surface, a message appeared!

Charlotte read the rhyme aloud:

"Two wishes need granting before
Christmas Day.
Help Tyra and Bethany without delay!"

Mia clutched Charlotte's hands. "Maybe we can break the spell on Ella and Alice, after all!" she said.

Charlotte glanced at the frozen princesses. "Of course we can," she said, her chin jutting out in determination. "We'll break the curse no matter what Princess Poison does."

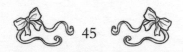

Together, Mia and Charlotte touched the ice again. Glowing pink and green light swirled around them. Charlotte fizzed with excitement as the magic whisked them through the air. *It's like travelling through a firework display,* she thought, as the Northern Lights danced around her.

A moment later, they landed in a room with mirrors along one wall. Glimpsing her reflection, Charlotte saw that she and Mia were wearing black leotards, like the other girls in the room. Because of how the magic worked, nobody noticed Mia and Charlotte's sudden appearance. The dancers were all busy practising ballet positions and stretching.

"Can you see Bethany and Tyra?" whispered Mia.

"There they are!" said Charlotte, spotting the two girls. They were doing pliés at a barre in the middle of the room. The girl with black hair caught them staring and smiled, revealing a mouthful of shiny silver braces.

"Do you want to use the barre?" she asked.

"Thanks," said Charlotte. She held on to the wooden barre and bent her legs deep at the knee. Mia did the same.

"Are you auditioning for the solo in the Christmas dance show?" the blonde girl asked them, peering at them anxiously through her pink-framed glasses.

"Er, no," stammered Mia.

The blonde girl looked relieved. "I'm Bethany," she said.

"And I'm Tyra," said the dark-haired girl.

"Hello," said Charlotte. "I'm Charlotte and this is my best friend, Mia."

"We're best friends, too!" exclaimed Tyra.

Bethany nodded. "We've been taking classes together since we were two!"

"We do ballet, tap and jazz," added Tyra. "Ballet's my favourite, but Bethany loves jazz."

"You must be really good dancers," said Mia.

"That's the problem," said Bethany, looking at Tyra miserably. "There's only one soloist in the Christmas show this year, and we're both trying out …"

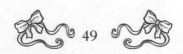

"It's horrible to compete with your best friend," said Tyra sadly.

"That's tough," said Charlotte sympathetically. She and Mia had very different interests, but she could imagine how hard it would be to compete against each other.

"I wish I could get the solo," said Bethany. "I've worked so hard this year."

"Me too," Tyra said. "I really wish I could be the soloist."

Mia and Charlotte exchanged puzzled looks. Before, when they'd granted a double wish, it was two different wishes – but Bethany and Tyra had the same wish! How were they ever going to make them both happy?

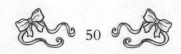

Bethany and Tyra turned away from each other, looking upset. Just then, a tall, thin woman in a long skirt entered the room. Her brown hair was scraped back in a tight bun, but her grey eyes were kind. She clapped her hands.

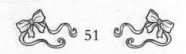

"I hope you've all warmed up," she said. "Come into the hall now."

"Yes, Miss Anastasia," said the girls, curtseying to their dance teacher.

Mia and Charlotte followed the dancers into the hall. It was decorated for Christmas, with tinsel garlands and a Christmas tree near the entrance.

"This year's show is set in the Land of Sweets," Miss Anastasia told the dancers. "It will showcase all the different styles of dance you study."

Excited chatter rippled among the dancers. Miss Anastasia held up a hand and her students quickly quietened down. "Everyone will dance in the show," the dance teacher continued. "But only one soloist will be chosen to play the part of the Christmas Fairy."

Bethany and Tyra crossed their arms over their chests, avoiding each other's eyes.

"The soloist must be skilled at ballet, tap and jazz," Miss Anastasia explained. "I'm looking for a dancer with excellent technique, who learns choreography quickly and dances with expression." Miss Anastasia switched on the sound system and a pop song started to play. "Enough talking," said the teacher. "Let's dance!"

"That's Alice's new Christmas song!" said Charlotte, recognising the melody. She felt a stab of worry as she remembered Alice, frozen by the Enchanted Lake. "We've got to grant

two wishes," she whispered to Mia. "But how? Bethany and Tyra both wished for the same thing."

"I know," said Mia. "It's impossible. There's only one Christmas Fairy and they both wish that they could be her."

Before Charlotte could reply, Miss Anastasia called, "Everyone on stage!"

Not wanting to stick out, Mia and Charlotte joined the dancers on stage. Miss Anastasia taught them a short, jazzy routine to Alice's song. After the teacher ran through the routine a few times, it was time for her students to do it on their own.

"Good luck, everyone!" Miss Anastasia said, smiling encouragingly.

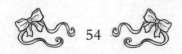

As she and Mia shimmied and sashayed in the back row of dancers, Charlotte kept an eye on Bethany and Tyra, who were at the front.

Both girls were brilliant dancers, but they seemed determined to outdo each other. Bethany stretched out her arms out so wide she knocked into Tyra. In return, her friend gave a high kick that nearly hit Bethany. Then they both leaped high into the air.

BUMP!

Bethany and Tyra collided and fell on their bottoms.

Oh dear, thought Charlotte. At this rate, neither of them would be the Christmas Fairy!

As the song came to an end, Charlotte did jazz hands and a flash of blue caught her eye – her sapphire ring was glowing.

Danger was near!

CHAPTER FOUR
Perfect Ballerinas

"Mia!" Charlotte whispered. "My ring is flashing!"

"Mine, too," said Mia.

They scanned the hall, looking for danger, but nothing seemed wrong.

"Well done, all of you," said Miss Anastasia. "That was fantastic dancing. Next we'll do the ballet audition in two smaller groups."

Half of the dancers remained on the stage, while the others sat down to watch, chatting excitedly. But Bethany and Tyra didn't look happy at all. They marched into the rehearsal room, glaring at each other.

"You crashed into me on purpose," Bethany accused her best friend. "You're so clumsy you don't deserve to be the Christmas Fairy."

"It was your fault," retorted Tyra. "You were showing off, as usual!"

Fuming, the two dancers turned their backs on each other as they took off their black jazz shoes and put on pink ballet slippers. Charlotte went over to Bethany while Mia went to comfort Tyra.

"Come on, you guys," Charlotte said

seriously. "Don't let the solo come between you."

"Is being the Christmas Fairy really more important than your friendship?" Mia asked.

A short, tubby cleaner in blue overalls with a big key ring dangling from his belt came into the rehearsal room, wheeling a trolley loaded with cleaning supplies.

The cleaner emptied a bin, then pushed the trolley into a small changing room.

"Yoo hoo! Girls!" he called. "I've found something that belongs to you."

Even though it was slightly muffled, his voice sounded familiar to Charlotte. Where did she know it from?

"Go and see what it is, Bethany," said Tyra.

"Stop bossing me around!" said Bethany.

"Fine! We'll both go!" huffed Tyra.

 As Bethany and Tyra stomped into the changing room, Charlotte's sapphire ring flashed again, even brighter than before.

"That's no cleaner!" she cried. "It's Hex!"

Hex was Princess Poison's nasty assistant, who helped her to spoil wishes.

Charlotte and Mia ran into the changing room. Hex had trapped Bethany and Tyra in the corner, blocking them in with his trolley.

"What a shame," he snarled. "You're going to miss your ballet audition."

"Oh no they aren't," said Charlotte.

"That's right," said Mia. "Because we're here to grant their wishes."

"Well, I hate to pour cold water on that idea," said Hex, "but ..." He lifted a bucket of dirty water from the cleaning trolley and threw it over Bethany and Tyra.

SPLASH!

The two dancers gasped in shock as the cold water hit them. Dirty water streamed down their faces and their leotards. They were drenched!

Hex dashed out of the room, slamming the door behind him.

Mia heard a key turning in a lock. "Hey!" she cried, pounding on the door. "Let us out!"

Charlotte banged on the door too. "Help!"

Loud piano music was coming from the audition in the hall. It drowned out their shouts.

"Why did you make me come in here?" Tyra snapped at Bethany. "Now we're going to miss the audition."

"You're probably glad we're trapped," Bethany shot back. "That way I won't get the solo!"

"Stop it!" shouted Mia. "Arguing isn't going to get us out of here."

"What *is* going to get us out of here?" muttered Charlotte. She pushed her shoulder against the door and tried to force it open. It wouldn't budge. Frustrated, she shook her head. "I guess we'll have to use a wish," she said, holding her glowing pendant.

"Wait!" said Mia. "I've got an idea. It might work, and then we wouldn't have to use up a wish."

Their necklaces only had enough magic to grant three small wishes for every person they

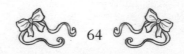

needed to help, so they had to use them wisely.

"I need a hairpin," said Mia.

Bethany pulled a hairpin out of her bedraggled bun. Mia bent the hairpin in half, making a lever. She eased it into the lock.

"What are you doing?" Bethany asked.

"This how you pick a lock," explained Mia. "I read how to do it in a library book about spies. Can I have another hairpin, please?"

Tyra gave one of her hairpins to Mia. "Does it really work?" she asked anxiously.

"We'll see," said Mia. She prised the second hairpin open and slid one end into the lock, wiggling it around.

Everyone looked on curiously as Mia tried to get the lock to turn. Her forehead furrowed

in concentration, Mia wriggled the hairpin inside the lock until …

CLICK!

"Here goes," Mia said.

Charlotte held her breath as Mia turned the door handle.

CREAK!

The door suddenly swung open!

"You did it!" whooped Charlotte. "Mia, you're a genius!"

"I can't believe it worked!" Mia squealed.

"Thanks so much!" said Tyra.

A flourish of piano music came from the hall, followed by applause.

"The first group must have finished their audition," said Bethany. "We got out just in time!"

"Oh no!" gasped Tyra, her hands flying to her mouth. "Look at us!"

Bethany and Tyra stared at their reflections in the rehearsal room mirrors. Their leotards and tights were dirty and sopping wet. Their buns were dishevelled, damp strands of hair falling around their faces. And, worst of all, when they walked over to the mirror to take a closer look, their ballet slippers made a horrid squelching sound. They couldn't possibly dance in them!

"Miss Anastasia says that ballerinas must always look graceful and elegant," said Bethany, dismayed. "Neither of us will get the solo looking like this!"

"Next group, take your places, please," called Miss Anastasia from the hall.

Tyra buried her face in her hands. "It's no use even trying."

"Hey," said Bethany, putting her arm around her friend's shoulders comfortingly. "We can't give up now – we've both worked too hard."

"That's right!" said Charlotte. "We can help you!" She turned to Mia. "Now can we use a wish?"

Mia nodded. It was time to do some magic!

Charlotte held her pendant against Mia's.

The two halves formed a glowing heart that lit up Charlotte's face as she said, "I wish that Bethany and Tyra looked like perfect ballerinas!"

CHAPTER FIVE
On Point

There was a flash of golden light and
Bethany and Tyra's soggy outfits were
magically transformed. Now they both wore
pale-pink leotards with wraparound cardigans,
floaty skirts and legwarmers. Mia and
Charlotte's clothes had changed into pretty
pink ballerina outfits too!

"Oh my gosh!" exclaimed Bethany, adjusting

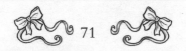

her glasses to peer at her new outfit.

"How did you do that?" asked Tyra, touching her hair, which was piled on top of her head in an elaborate bun.

"Go!" Charlotte ordered them. "We'll explain later. You don't want to be late for your ballet audition."

"Good luck!" Mia called as they pattered out of the rehearsal room in brand-new ballet slippers.

Mia and Charlotte went into the hall so they could watch the girls audition. As piano music played, Miss Anastasia called out instructions to the dancers.

"Second position!"

The dancers stepped their feet apart and held their arms out to the side.

"Fifth position!"

The dancers crossed their feet and raised their arms above their head.

"Arabesque!"

The dancers lifted their legs high in the air.

As Miss Anastasia continued to call out ballet moves, Charlotte watched Bethany and Tyra perform jetés, pliés and pirouettes. Both girls were graceful and had excellent technique, but they kept sneaking sideways glances at each other. While the other dancers had big smiles on their faces, Bethany and Tyra looked tense.

"Oh dear," Charlotte said. "They don't look like they're having fun."

"They're too worried about getting the solo," said Mia.

"At least they haven't crashed into each other this time," said Charlotte.

When the second group of dancers had finished their audition, Miss Anastasia said, "Well done. We'll move on to the tap audition next.

I'm going to put you in twos." Miss Anastasia paired up dancers. "Tyra and Bethany," she said. "You dance together."

Bethany groaned.

Tyra glared at her. "I don't want to dance with you either!"

"Because you know I'll make you look bad," Bethany said, narrowing her eyes.

"They're arguing again," sighed Mia. "I don't see how we're even going to even grant one wish at this rate."

"Let's go and sort it out," said Charlotte, striding over to the dancers. "Otherwise we won't be able to help Alice and Ella."

When they saw Mia and Charlotte approaching, Tyra and Bethany suddenly stopped quarrelling.

"How did you change our clothes?" Tyra asked them eagerly.

"You've got to tell us," said Bethany. "I'm dying to know."

"If we explain, do you promise to stop arguing?" said Mia.

Tyra and Bethany gave each other sideways looks.

"I guess so," said Bethany, shrugging.

Tyra nodded reluctantly.

"OK," said Mia. "We'll tell you."

"It was magic!" said Charlotte.

Bethany and Tyra turned to each other, their eyes wide. Then they both squealed with excitement.

"We're training to become Secret Princesses," explained Charlotte. "Our necklaces let us do magic. We came here to help make your wishes come true – but it has to be a secret. Do you promise not to tell anyone?"

"We pinky promise!" said Tyra. She and Bethany both linked their little fingers and shook on it.

"This is so awesome," said Bethany, her eyes shining behind her glasses.

"How did you get picked to become Secret Princesses?" asked Tyra.

"It's because our friendship is really strong," said Mia. "We're training to become a special type of Secret Princess called Friendship Princesses."

"We always work together," said Charlotte.

"You're so lucky," said Bethany, sighing wistfully. "I'd love to be able to do magic."

"We are lucky," said Mia. "But so are you. And you've already got something magical."

"What do you mean?" Tyra asked, confused.

"Your friendship," said Mia.

"Friends make you stronger," said Charlotte.

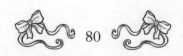

"If you work together, you can make all your dreams come true."

Tyra and Bethany looked at each other sheepishly.

"I'm sorry I haven't been a good friend lately," Tyra told Bethany. "And for the mean things I said."

"Me too," said Bethany. "We shouldn't have let the solo come between us."

The two girls gave each other a big hug.

"I'm glad we're doing

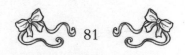

the tap dance audition together," said Tyra.

"Me too," said Bethany. "You're the best dancer I know!"

"Hurry up and put on your tap shoes!" urged Charlotte.

Bethany and Tyra quickly changed from their soft ballet slippers into tap shoes with low heels. They went back out to the hall, their arms around each other's shoulders.

"Aw!" said Charlotte. "I'm glad they're getting along now."

When it was Tyra and Bethany's turn to audition, they launched into an energetic tap dance routine. Smiling broadly, their feet started moving in perfect time, their toes making tippety-tap sounds to the music.

"Uh oh," groaned Mia.

"What?" asked Charlotte. "They're dancing really well."

"Hex is back," said Mia.

Hex wheeled his cleaner's trolley into the hall noisily, trying to distract the dancers. It didn't work – Bethany and Tyra were totally focussed on their dancing.

Hex scowled and took a spray bottle from his trolley. Going up close to the stage, he squirted the bottle and pretended to clean the wall.

AAACHOOOO! Tyra sneezed.

AAACHOOOO! Bethany sneezed as well.

"What's he done?" said Mia.

Hex pushed the cleaning trolley over to Mia and Charlotte. "This should SPICE things up!" he said, waving the bottle at them. "It's pepper spray!"

AAACHOOOO!
AAACHOOOO!
AAACHOOOO! Tyra
and Bethany couldn't
stop sneezing. Their
eyes were streaming,
but they both kept on
dancing.

"They won't be
getting the solo now,"
said Hex smugly, wheeling his trolley away.

"We've got to help them!" Mia said.

She and Charlotte held their pendants
together. "I wish for the pepper to change
to … PEPPERMINT!" Mia blurted out.

All of a sudden, Tyra and Bethany were

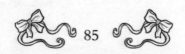

holding big red and white striped peppermint candy canes!

The dancers didn't miss a beat. They twirled their candy canes, then held them overhead and kicked their from legs side to side. Grinning, Tyra and Bethany tossed their peppermint canes back and forth to each other.

They finished by planting their canes on the ground and jumping up, clicking their heels together.

Everyone watching burst into applause. Thanks to the magic, nobody had noticed anything strange when the canes appeared.

"Fantastic!" Miss Anastasia said. "Well done everyone. Right, now cool down and then gather around." The class all worked through a final series of exercises and then all sat on the floor in front of their teacher. Charlotte and Mia went too, Charlotte's tummy twisting nervously. Was Miss Anastasia going to announce the soloists?

"I've seen some wonderful dancing today," said Miss Anastasia. "I haven't chosen a

soloist yet, but I have narrowed it down to two finalists: Bethany ..."

Bethany yelped with joy as Tyra threw her arms around her.

Decision Time

"… and Tyra!"

Tyra's face broke into a huge grin, showing her shiny braces. "We're the final two!" she squealed. But her excitement faded as she realised something. "But only one of us is going to be the Christmas Fairy."

Mia and Charlotte glanced at each other, exchanging worried looks. Uh oh. Would

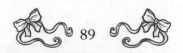

Bethany and Tyra start arguing with each other again?

"It's OK," Bethany said. "I'll be happy if you get the solo, Tyra."

"Same here," said Tyra. "You'd be a brilliant Christmas Fairy."

"To help me choose, I'd like you each to do a freestyle dance of your choice," Miss Anastasia announced.

"Do you want to go first?" Bethany offered.

"Thanks," said Tyra, letting out a deep breath. "I'd like to get it over with."

In the rehearsal room, Tyra changed out of her tap shoes. She put the ballet slippers she'd worn earlier back on.

Mia, Charlotte and Bethany watched from

the wings as Tyra danced across the stage, as graceful as a swan.

"She's an amazing ballerina," said Bethany.

A sharp fingernail tapped Charlotte on the shoulder. She turned and came face to face with Princess Poison.

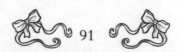

"Is your ballerina friend good at ice skating too?" Princess Poison asked slyly.

"I don't know," said Charlotte as Mia pulled her away.

"Well, let's find out," said Princess Poison. She pointed her wand at the stage and said:

"Mess with me and you'll pay the price.
Make the dance floor turn into ice!"

Green light flew from her wand and hit the stage floor.

"Whoa!" said Tyra, losing her balance as she pirouetted. Her arms windmilled and her feet slid clumsily, like someone ice skating for the first time.

"Uh oh, looks like someone's wish is on thin ice," sneered Princess Poison, sauntering off.

"Do something!" Bethany begged Mia and Charlotte. "Please!"

Charlotte glanced down at her pendant. It was glowing very weakly now, but there was just enough magic to make one more wish.

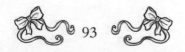

She and Mia formed a heart with their pendants.

"I wish for the floor to go back to normal," Charlotte said.

The ice vanished and Tyra finished her dance with a series of huge jumps.

"That was brilliant," said Bethany, hugging her friend as she came off stage.

"Are you sure?" Tyra asked breathlessly. "Something weird happened to the floor."

They hurried into the rehearsal room so Bethany could get ready.

"Oh no," groaned Charlotte.

"Oh yes," said Princess Poison, swinging Bethany's jazz shoes around by their laces. "You have no magic left to stop me now."

She pointed her
wand and said:

**"Princess Poison won't
be beat,
Give this dancer two
left feet!"**

Green magic
flowed from her wand
to Bethany's shoes,
then Princess Poison
threw them on the
ground.

"You're horrible!"
Mia said.

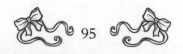

"If the shoe fits, wear it," said Princess Poison, shrugging nonchalantly. Bethany tried to put her shoes on. The left shoe fit, but she couldn't stuff her right foot into the other shoe.

"I can't dance in two left shoes," she said.

"Oh no," gasped Princess Poison, feigning concern. "You shan't go to the ball!" Smirking at Mia and Charlotte, she added, "And neither will the Secret Princesses." Then she waved her wand and vanished with a flash of green light.

Bethany's shoulders slumped sadly. "Who *is*

that mean lady?" she asked.

"Her name is Princess Poison," said Charlotte. "She used to be a Secret Princess, but now she uses her magic to spoil wishes."

"I wish we could help you," said Mia, placing her hand on Bethany's shoulder. "But we've used up all our magic."

"She doesn't need magic," said Tyra. She handed Bethany a pair of jazz shoes. "Our feet are the same size," she said. "You can borrow my shoes!"

"Are you sure?" Bethany asked.

"Of course," said Tyra selflessly. "Good luck."

Bethany put on Tyra's shoes then hurried onstage to do her final audition. Snapping her fingers, she strutted along to a jazzy pop song.

Sassy and spirited, her movements perfectly conveyed the music's emotion. To finish, she arched her back and kicked her leg high in the air, then dropped on to the floor.

"That was fantastic," said Mia.

Tyra nodded. "Bethany's brilliant at jazz."

"It was really kind to loan Bethany your shoes," said Charlotte.

"She's my best friend," said Tyra. "I'd do anything for her."

"That's what Princess Poison can't understand," said Mia. "Friendship is stronger than any magic."

Tyra went onstage and gave Bethany a big hug. Miss Anastasia gazed at them thoughtfully.

"Girls," she said eventually, "I've made my decision about the soloist."

A hush fell over all the dancers as they waited for Miss Anastasia's verdict. Charlotte's tummy churned nervously and Mia grabbed her arm. No matter who Miss Anastasia picked, one girl was going to be disappointed.

So how could she and Mia make both their wishes come true?

"You're both wonderful dancers," Miss Anastasia said. "But the best dance you did was your tap audition, when you danced together."

Tyra reached out and took Bethany's hand.

"I can't decide between you, so this year we'll have two soloists," said Miss Anastasia. "Tyra and Bethany will *both* be our Christmas Fairies!"

"This is incredible," Tyra said, shaking her head in disbelief. "My wish came true!"

"Mine too!" said Bethany, tears of joy trickling down her cheeks.

The lights on the Christmas tree at the back of the hall started to twinkle. The fairy on

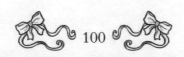

the top came to life and fluttered into the air.
Charlotte and Mia grinned. They knew the
magic was because they had granted Bethany
AND Tyra's wish!

The fairy flew around the hall, leaving a trail
of sparkles hovering in the air.

"She's writing a
message," whispered
Mia.

"*Return to
Wishing Star
Palace!*" Charlotte
read aloud. Their
ruby slippers had
magically appeared
on their feet.

"Excuse me," said Charlotte, guiding Mia through the crowd of dancers congratulating Tyra and Bethany. "We've got to go now," she told them. "Good luck with your show."

"Thanks for making our wish come true," said Bethany. "Will you come back and see the show on Christmas Eve?"

Mia and Charlotte exchanged uncertain looks. They had granted both girls' wishes so they probably wouldn't be coming back. "We will if we can," said Charlotte.

"Please come," Tyra urged them. "We wouldn't have got the solos without your help. I really wish the show would be amazing."

Bethany nodded. "Me too. I wish it could be the best Christmas dance show ever!"

Waving goodbye, Mia and Charlotte clicked the heels of their ruby slippers three times and said, "The Enchanted Lake!"

WHOOSH! A moment later they were by the lake, under a night sky billowing with yellow and green light. Alice and Ella stood frozen like ice sculptures.

"They're moving!" shouted Mia.

The princesses were beginning to move stiffly. "Aaaah," Ella said, stretching her arms over her head. "That's better."

"Thanks, girls," Alice said, coming to give them a hug. "You saved us! Let's get back to the palace and warm up."

They held hands and clicked their heels – but when they arrived in front of the palace they had a horrible shock. It was still completely frozen.

"But why is the palace still frozen?" asked Mia, puzzled. "We granted Bethany and Tyra's wishes. They both got to be Christmas Fairies."

"Hmm," said Ella. "But it was the same wish. maybe that only counts as one. They must

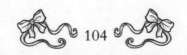

have another wish that you need to grant to
break the curse on the palace."

"They did both wish for the dance show to
be amazing," said Charlotte. "But it isn't until
Christmas Eve."

"Then you'll need to come back here in a few
weeks," said Alice. "To grant their second wish
on Christmas Eve – just in time for the ball."

"We'll grant the next wish," said Charlotte. "I
promise."

"Pinky promise?" asked Mia.

"Pinky promise," confirmed Charlotte.

The girls linked their little fingers and shook
on it. Then Ella waved her wand and Charlotte
felt herself soaring past the Northern Lights,
the glowing colours swirling around her.

A moment later she was back in her kitchen. Thanks to the magic, no time had passed while she had been away. Charlotte ran back outside, just in time to see her dad switch on the Christmas lights.

"Ta da!" he said.

"They look great, Dad," said Charlotte. The light-up Santa waved his arm and the reindeer's red nose flashed.

"I can't wait for Santa to come," said Liam.

"Me neither," said Harvey.

Charlotte was excited about Santa's visit too, but this year she had something else to look forward to on Christmas Eve – granting another wish with Mia!

Story Two

CHAPTER ONE
A Snowy Surprise

"Jingle bells, jingle bells, jingle all the way!"
sang Charlotte and her brothers as they drove
home on Christmas Eve. Charlotte's family had
spent the afternoon at the beach, building a
Santa-shaped sand sculpture and decorating a
seaweed Christmas tree with seashells.

"Home sweet home!" said Charlotte's mum
as her dad pulled the car into their driveway.

The fairy lights in the garden twinkled invitingly and there was a pretty wreath hanging on their front door.

As they all piled out of the car, Liam and Harvey peered up at the sky.

"Is that it?" Liam asked, pointing up at a flashing light.

"I think that's just an aeroplane," said Harvey, squinting.

"What are you looking for?" Charlotte asked her brothers.

"Santa's sleigh," said Liam.

"Santa won't come until we're asleep, silly," Charlotte said. She glanced down at her pendant, but it wasn't glowing yet. All day long she'd been checking it, wondering when she could go back to Wishing Star Palace. Time was running out to break Princess Poison's curse!

"Come inside, kids," said Charlotte's mum. "The sooner you go to bed, the sooner it will be Christmas."

"OK!" The twins ran inside excitedly.

As she went indoors, Charlotte breathed in the delicious aroma of mince pies. They'd baked a batch before going to the beach.

"Mmm," said Dad, picking up a pie and taking a big bite.

"Stop, Dad!" Harvey said. "Those are for Santa!"

"Don't worry," said Mum, chuckling. "There are plenty for us, too."

Charlotte bit into a mince pie. It tasted as good as it smelled!

"Yum!" said Liam, spraying crumbs. "These are so good."

"Mia sent me the recipe," said Charlotte. Her best friend was brilliant at baking. She and Mia messaged each other all the time, but

it had been a few weeks since they had seen each other – since they had magially granted Bethany and Tyra's first wish. Charlotte glanced down at her necklace again. This time it was glowing!

"I'm going to go and get into my pyjamas," Charlotte said, quickly swallowing the last of her mince pie.

She hurried to her bedroom and shut the door. Holding her pendant, she said, "I wish I could see Mia!"

Light from the pendant filled the room
and swept Charlotte away.

"Merry Christmas!" a voice greeted
her as she landed in the hallway at
Wishing Star Palace.

Charlotte turned and saw Mia by a staircase covered in a carpet of snow. Icicles hung down from the ceilings and chandeliers, and every surface glittered with a thick layer of frost.

Charlotte hugged Mia. Like Charlotte, Mia was wearing her princess dress, tiara and ruby slippers.

Princess Ella came through the front door, her cheeks rosy. "Thanks for coming, girls. I've just been checking on the animals in the stables."

PLOP!

A drop of cold water fell onto Charlotte's nose. "The icicles are dripping," she said, looking up.

"I know, and it's very bad for my instruments

to be so damp," Princess Alice said, coming down the stairs. "But at least *I'm* not an icicle any more, since you made Tyra and Bethany's first wish come true!"

"Can we grant their second wish now?" Charlotte asked eagerly. If they granted another wish the palace would be unfrozen – just in time for the magical masked ball.

"Not until my wand glows," said Ella.

Charlotte sighed. "I hate waiting."

"Why don't we decorate the palace?" suggested Mia. "It might be frozen, but it can still be ready for the ball."

"That's a great idea," said Ella.

Alice waved her wand and magically gave the girls warm coats, hats and boots. Then

Ella led them to a copse of trees, where two reindeer were grazing in a clearing under the branches.

"It's Joy and Noelle!" cried Mia.

"They came back!" said Charlotte.

"Of course they did," said Ella, scratching Noelle behind the antlers. "Reindeer always find their way home."

Ella, Alice, Mia and Charlotte gathered
armfuls of fragrant pine boughs and prickly
holly studded with crimson berries. They
carried the evergreens back to the palace,
then Mia and Charlotte began arranging pine
boughs on the mantelpiece.

"I've got a better idea," said Ella. She waved
her wand and suddenly garlands of pine and

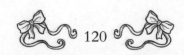

holly hung all over the palace.

"It looks gorgeous!" said Mia.

As Ella flicked her wand again, adding baubles and gold bows to the garlands, Charlotte noticed something. "Ella! Your wand is glowing!"

"Quick, to the magic mirror!" Ella said.

"Good luck!" Alice called as the girls clicked the heels of their ruby slippers.

The turret room was so cold that the girls' breath came out in clouds. Mia read the message on the icy glass:

"Grant one more wish before Christmas Day
To make Princess Poison's curse melt away!"

The girls touched the ice and a flurry of snowflakes swirled up around them. The magical snowflakes swept Mia and Charlotte back to the dance hall, where a dress rehearsal was taking place. The stage looked very different from how it had during the auditions. There was a gingerbread house with a fence made of big candy canes and giant lollipops. On either side of the house stood two beautifully decorated Christmas trees.

"Wow!" said Mia. "The set looks fantastic."

"So do the dancers," said Charlotte. "They've obviously been working really hard these past few weeks."

The dancers were performing to Alice's song, *Christmas Dream*, played by a band

of musicians by the side of the stage. It was the same routine that Mia and Charlotte had performed at the audition. "Now, time for the big finish with our two Christmas Fairies!" Miss Anastasia called out. At the end of the song a few of the dancers lifted two familiar girls up into the air. It was Tyra and Bethany!

Miss Anastasia clapped her hands. "That was fantastic," she said. "I know you'll make me very proud tonight."

As the dancers headed backstage to get ready for the show, Tyra and Bethany spotted Mia and Charlotte.

"You came!" cried Tyra, running over.

"We can't wait to see the show," said Charlotte.

"How do you feel?" Mia asked them.

"Nervous," said Bethany. "But excited too. My one wish is for the show to be wonderful."

Tyra nodded. "I really wish it goes well tonight too, so we can make everyone proud. Miss Anastasia has worked so hard, and our parents made the sets and costumes."

"Well, we're going to help make your wish come true!" Mia said with a grin.

"I'm sure the show will be amazing," Charlotte said. *As long as Princess Poison doesn't try to spoil it*, she added silently ...

CHAPTER TWO
Costume Drama

"Do you want to come backstage with us?"
Tyra asked them.

"Sure," said Mia. "We can help you get
ready."

Tyra and Bethany led them backstage to a
dressing room. There was a mirror surrounded
by bright light bulbs and a clothes rail with
tutus hanging from it.

"We got our own dressing room because we're the soloists," Bethany explained proudly.

"How do you want your hair?" Charlotte asked Tyra.

"In a bun, please," said Tyra.

Charlotte had been in lots of dance recitals, so she knew what to do. She sprayed water on Tyra's long, dark hair and brushed it to get the tangles out. Copying her, Mia dampened Bethany's fair hair and brushed it until it was silky smooth.

Next, they made ponytails at the nape of each girl's neck.

"I feel like a real hairdresser," said Charlotte.

"You're good at this," Bethany told Mia as she twisted the ponytail into a coil.

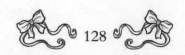

"Thanks," said Mia, pinning Bethany's bun in place. "Sometimes I play with my little sister's hair." She aimed a can of glitter hairspray at Bethany's hair.

PSSSSSTTTT!

Slicked back smoothly, Bethany's blonde hair glittered with hairspray. Mia passed the can to Charlotte.

PSSSSSTTTT! Charlotte sprayed Tyra's hair, making it sparkle. "Even a gale force wind won't mess up your hair now," joked Charlotte.

"Now for the finishing touch," said Mia, placing a tiara on Bethany's head.

Charlotte put a matching tiara on Tyra. "You two look like Secret Princesses."

"Do you have tiaras too?" Tyra asked them.

"Yes," Mia said. "But we only wear them at Wishing Star Palace."

"That's so cool," said Bethany.

"Can you help us with our make-up?" Tyra asked.

Bethany took off her glasses so Mia could brush blue eyeshadow on her eyelids, while Charlotte powdered Tyra's cheeks with rosy

pink blusher.

"There," said
Charlotte,
painting bright
red lipstick on
both girls' lips.
"Now even people at
the back will be able to
see your smiles."

Their make-up done, Tyra and Bethany
changed into white tutus.

"You look beautiful," said Mia.

"Our costumes for the finale are even more
gorgeous," said Tyra, showing her two pink
tutus hanging on the clothes rail. "My mum
made them."

Just then there was a knock on the dressing room door.

"I'll get it," said Charlotte. She opened the door and saw a massive bunch of lilies.

"Delivery for Tyra and Bethany," said the delivery man, his face hidden by the huge bouquet.

"That is so nice," said Tyra. "I wonder who sent them."

As Tyra and Bethany went to the door, the delivery man thrust the flowers straight at them.

"They're from Princess Poison," Hex said. "She says break a leg."

"Oh no!" said Tyra, looking down in horror. Her white tutu was covered in bright orange pollen from the lilies. Bethany's tutu was covered in orange powder too.

Mia plucked a tissue from the make-up table and tried to rub the pollen off. It just smeared and made the stain worse!

"Someone needs to sign for the delivery," said Hex. He grabbed the red lipstick and scrawled his name on each of the pink tutus hanging on the clothes rail.

"You've ruined our costumes!" shrieked Tyra.

"Get used to it," said Hex. "Because Princess Poison is going to ruin the whole show!"

Laughing nastily, he threw down the lipstick and left.

"Don't worry," Mia assured Tyra and Bethany. "We won't let anyone spoil the show."

"But we can't dance in these ..." said Bethany, looking down at her stained tutu.

Charlotte and Mia put their glowing pendants together. As light shone from the heart, Charlotte said, "I wish Bethany and Tyra had the most beautiful costumes ever."

There was a flash of light and Bethany and Tyra's tutus were transformed. Their new costumes were bright white, with layers of soft tulle. The bodices were embellished with snowflakes made of tiny crystals. Attached to

each girl's back were gauzy fairy wings. Now they really were Christmas Fairies!

"Oh, wow!" said Tyra, admiring her tutu in the mirror. When she twirled, something even more amazing happened – tiny lights in the tutu twinkled and her fairy wings fluttered!

"This is amazing," said Bethany. She pirouetted, lighting up her own skirt.

Charlotte held up a pretty pink tutu. "These are fixed, too." There was no trace of Hex's greasy scrawl any more. The new costumes for the finale had puffed sleeves and silver flowers embroidered on them.

"Won't my mum be confused because the costumes look different?" Tyra asked.

Mia shook her head. "Only you two will notice the magic."

"Thank you so much!" Tyra bounced on her toes. "I'm too excited to stay still."

"Let's do some stretches," Bethany said.

They joined the other dancers in the rehearsal room, where they were warming up

to pop music. As Bethany and Tyra stretched their legs at the barre, one of Alice's songs started to play.

"We've got to grant their second wish," Mia whispered. "Not just for them – for the princesses too. They deserve to have a brilliant Christmas ball."

"We will," Charlotte said. "We'll do everything we can to make sure the show is amazing."

Miss Anastasia entered the rehearsal room. "Ten minutes until show time, girls."

The dancers squealed with excitement.

Miss Anastasia smiled and put a finger to her lips. "I'm going to open the house doors soon, so keep the noise down."

"Would you like us to be ushers?" Mia
offered. "We could show people to their seats."

"Thanks," said Miss Anastasia. "That would
be very helpful."

Mia and Charlotte went into the hall, where
folding chairs had been set up in rows. Two
flashes of blue light caught Charlotte's eye.
At first she thought it was from the Christmas
trees onstage, but then, with a sinking feeling,
she realised where the light was coming from.

"Oh no," Charlotte groaned. "Our rings are
glowing again!"

CHAPTER THREE
Sweet to Sour

"Princess Poison is going to try and spoil the show," said Mia, twisting her sapphire ring anxiously.

"We won't let her," said Charlotte.

"Hasn't anyone ever told you it's rude to talk about someone behind their back?" said Princess Poison, appearing in front of them.

"You should know," Charlotte retorted.

"You're the rudest person I know."

Princess Poison laughed. "Feeling feisty, are you? Your little friend is right – I am going to spoil the show."

"No you're not," said Mia. "You didn't spoil their first wish and you're not going to spoil their second wish either."

Princess Poison scowled. "One wish doesn't count for anything – it takes two to break my curse. I hope the princesses wanted a white Christmas, because Wishing Star Palace is going to be frozen solid – for ever!" Narrowing

her cold, green eyes, Princes Poison pointed her
wand at the stage and muttered a spell.

**"Make this Land of Sweets turn sour,
Spoil a wish to get more power!"**

Green light shot out of the wand and hit the
lovely set. Now the gingerbread house looked
like a ruin. The house was crumbling, the
windows were cracked and the candy fence was
falling down. All the needles had fallen off the
Christmas trees, leaving their branches bare.

"It's not so sweet now," Princess Poison
gloated.

"Why do you have to be so horrible?" Mia
cried out in frustration.

Princess Poison widened her eyes in mock innocence. "I was just doing you a favour," she said. "Sweets are bad for your teeth. I thought you goody-goodies would approve."

"Go away!" Charlotte ordered her. "You've done enough damage."

"I'm just getting started," hissed Princess Poison. "I'm going to ruin the lights, too." She pointed her wand at the ceiling and said:

**"Make the stage lights all fall down
Turn everyone's smile into a–"**

"Oh no you don't!" shouted Charlotte, running onstage before Princess Poison could finish the spell. She grabbed a giant lollipop

142

from the
set and
swung it,
trying to
knock the
wand out of
Princess Poison's
hand.

"So you want to play
rough ..." said Princess Poison.
She grabbed another giant lollipop
and advanced towards Charlotte, her eyes
glittering malevolently.

"Be careful, Charlotte!" cried Mia.

Princess Poison and Charlotte duelled,
holding the lollipop sticks like swords.

SWOOSH! Princess Poison lunged towards Charlotte, slicing her lollipop sword through the air. Charlotte neatly dodged her blow and Princess Poison whacked one of the Christmas trees instead.

SWASH! Charlotte tricked Princess Poison by pretending to go to the left, then lunged forward towards the right. She backed Princess

Poison against the gingerbread house.

"Drop your wand," Charlotte ordered her.

"OK, OK," said Princess Poison.
"I surrender." She bent down
to lay her wand on the
floor, but as soon as
Charlotte lowered
her lollipop, Princess
Poison snatched her
wand up.

"Ha! You're not
the only one who can
fake," Princess Poison
said. She pointed her
wand at the lights and
green magic exploded

overhead. The stage lights shattered with a loud *CRACK!* Broken glass rained down on to the stage.

"Charlotte!" cried Mia, rushing onstage to drag her friend out of harm's way. They huddled by the side of the stage, pulling the velvet stage curtains over them to shield themselves from falling glass.

"I need a rest. I'm shattered," said Princess Poison, laughing uproariously at her terrible joke. She waved her wand and vanished in a cloud of green smoke.

"She doesn't need a rest, she needs to be arrested," grumbled Charlotte.

"At least you haven't lost your sense of humour," Mia said wryly.

"Is everything OK?" called Tyra, running out from backstage. "We heard noises."

"Stop!" warned Charlotte, waving her arms. "Don't come any closer!" If the dancers stepped on the sharp glass, they might hurt their feet.

"Who did this?" Bethany said, staring at the ruined set and the glass shards littering the stage.

"Princess Poison," Charlotte said grimly. "Who else?"

"Our parents worked so hard to build that set," said Tyra, her voice quavering with distress.

They heard Miss Anastasia's voice outside the hall. "Come in! The house is now open." A key fumbled in a lock as the dance teacher opened the hall's doors.

"We need to fix this!" said Mia.

The girls held their pendants together and Mia said, "I wish the set and lighting were even better than before."

Dazzling light radiated from their necklaces and filled the stage. The crumbling gingerbread house was replaced with one that

looked just like Wishing Star Palace – except
it was made entirely of sweets! The roof tiles
looked like chocolate drops and the four turrets
were upside-down ice cream cones. Glittering
sweeties surrounded the heart-shaped windows
and stripy candy sticks framed the doorway.

The branches of the two Christmas trees were green once more, and shiny baubles shaped like sweets dangled from them.

The lights had been repaired, too. They cast a warm glow on the stage, changing from luminous pinks and purples to soft greens and yellows. The gorgeous colours reminded Charlotte of the Northern Lights.

"Wow!" said Tyra, gaping at the new set.

"Quick! Go backstage!" Mia said, shooing Bethany and Tyra away. "You don't want the audience to see you!"

"Good luck!" Charlotte called as she pulled the stage curtains shut.

People started to stream into the hall, so Mia and Charlotte hurried to the entrance and

handed out programmes.

"Enjoy the show!" said Charlotte, leading a mum with two boys to their seats in the front row. They all had fair hair and the mum had glasses, which made Charlotte guess that they were Bethany's family.

"Here are your seats," said Mia, showing a dark-haired couple to seats next to the blonde family. *Tyra's parents*, guessed Charlotte.

"This is such an exciting way to spend Christmas Eve," Bethany's mum said to Tyra's mum.

Catching Mia's eye, Charlotte winked. She couldn't have agreed more!

Once the audience had been seated, Miss Anastasia came onstage and thanked everyone

for coming. Then the lights dimmed, the band started to play and the curtains opened. The show was starting!

CHAPTER FOUR
Tuning Out

As the show began, Mia and Charlotte found
two empty seats at the side of the hall and
sat down. Miss Anastasia's youngest students
toddled on to the stage wearing red and white
tutus that made them look like cute little
peppermint sweeties. As the band played a
familiar Christmas carol, the little dancers
did cute pirouettes and pliés, though not all

at quite the same time.

"Ooooh!" cooed Mia. "They are so sweet."

"That's how we must have looked when we did baby ballet together," said Charlotte, giving Mia a squeeze.

One of the little dancers spotted her parents in the audience and waved, making the audience chuckle. When the tiny ballerinas finished with clumsy curtseys, everyone gave them a big round of applause.

Then Tyra and Bethany pattered onstage, the crystals on their white costumes reflected the soft colours of the stage lights. Rising on to the points of their ballet slippers, the Christmas Fairies performed a graceful duet. Their hands poised above their heads, they each extended a

leg high in the air and spun around on the tips of their toes.

"Oooh!" gasped the audience as the lights on the girls' tutus lit up.

Glancing over at Bethany and Tyra's parents, Charlotte could see their faces shining with pride as they watched their daughters perform onstage.

"They're doing brilliantly," Mia whispered.

Charlotte nodded. She crossed her fingers, hoping that nothing would go wrong.

For the next number, six girls dressed as gingerbread men did a tap dance. Charlotte couldn't help tapping her feet along to the lively music. At the end of the routine, Tyra and Bethany came back onstage in their tap shoes and did a short solo, kicking their legs out to the side and back in again as their arms circled in the air.

156

They moved so fast they almost looked like they were flying!

"Yay!" cheered Mia.

Charlotte stuck two fingers in her mouth and gave a loud wolf whistle. "That move is called wings," she whispered to Mia. "It's really hard to do."

The next performance was a jazz routine. The dancers wore black leotards with colourful skirts and hats shaped like liquorice allsorts. The two Christmas Fairies came leaping onstage to join in with the routine. Even from a distance Charlotte could see the huge smiles on Tyra and Bethany's faces.

"They're having lots of fun," she whispered to Mia happily.

The door at the back of the hall opened, letting in light as two latecomers arrived. Charlotte's heart sank when she turned and saw who it was. "Just what we didn't want for Christmas," she groaned.

"Excuse me," said Princess Poison, barging her way through a row of people to get to two empty seats.

"Coming through," said Hex, as people stood to let him squeeze past.

"I'm sure we haven't missed anything good," Princess Poison said loudly.

"Actually, the show is great," said Mia, glaring at her. "And you can't ruin it."

"Ooh," said Princess Poison. "A challenge."

She pointed her wand at the band and said a spell under her breath:

**"Make the band tuneless and play off-key,
Spoil the music so there's more power for me!"**

Green light streamed out of her wand and hit the piano, the drums, the violin and the trumpet. The song the band had been playing

suddenly
sounded
dreadful.

SCREECH! went
the violin.

BLATT! went the
trumpet.

PLONK! went the piano.

BLAM! went the drums.
The musicians carried
on playing, seeming
not to notice the
din they were
making. The
audience
winced

and covered their ears to block out the terrible racket.

Onstage, the dancers faltered. Bethany and Tyra exchanged worried looks as they struggled to keep their carefully choreographed steps in time to the band's random toots, bangs and squeals.

"Boo!" called Hex. "BOOOOO!"

"This show is rubbish," said Princess Poison. "Come on, Hex. We're leaving." They started making their way back along the row.

Charlotte held up her pendant. It was glowing very faintly, but they still had enough magic to make one more wish. It was the only way they could save the show – and make the girls' second wish come true.

She and Mia held their pendants together. "I wish the musicians would play in tune again," Charlotte said.

Light beamed from their necklaces and instantly the band was playing harmoniously. Relief flooding their faces, Tyra and Bethany continued their routine.

Thanks to the magic, no one else noticed anything strange. The dancers finished their routine with some impressive kicks and twirls as the audience beamed. Princess Poison and Hex, who were nearly at the exit, stopped and turned around. Shooting Mia and Charlotte a furious look, Princess Poison grabbed Hex's arm and marched to the front of the hall. They slipped through a door at the side of the stage.

"Oh no," Mia said. "They're going backstage! And we don't have any magic left!"

"That doesn't matter," said Charlotte, getting out of her seat. "We're not going to let them spoil the show!"

CHAPTER FIVE
Sleeping Beauties

Mia and Charlotte hurried through the stage door. They squeezed past a group of dancers dressed in shiny purple, pink and gold leotards who were trooping onstage, looking like brightly wrapped chocolates.

Mia and Charlotte hurried over to the soloists' dressing room. To their relief, Princess Poison and Hex weren't there. Bethany and

Tyra were changing into their costumes for the grand finale.

"Hi," said Bethany breathlessly. "Can you help me zip this up?"

Mia zipped up the back of her costume. "You look gorgeous."

They had pale pink dresses with floaty chiffon skirts and, of course, their glittery wings.

"What do you think of the show so far?" Tyra asked them anxiously.

"You two have been amazing," Charlotte answered truthfully. "It's going really well."

"Did you fix the music when it went all weird?" Bethany asked.

Mia nodded. "Don't worry – nobody else noticed."

"We're on again after the tap dancers," said Tyra. They went into the rehearsal room. Dancers were changing into pink and white tutus with poofy skirts.

"They look like marshmallows," said Mia in delight.

Just then, Charlotte caught sight of something much less sweet – Princess Poison and Hex.

"There they are," said Princess Poison, sidling

up to Tyra and Bethany.
"What a wonderful
performance you've been
giving. Honestly, I don't
know how you have any
energy left."

Hex giggled.

Charlotte wasn't sure
what Princess Poison was
planning, but she knew it
wouldn't be good.

Tyra looked puzzled.
"We're fine," she said.

"We only have one more

routine to do," said Bethany.

"I feel certain that you two could use a nap," insisted Princess Poison. She pulled out her wand and started hissing a spell:

"Make these dancers fall fast sleep
Don't let them make another—"

Before Princess Poison could finish the spell, Charlotte grabbed a tap shoe and flung it as hard as she could. It hit Princess Poison's wand,

knocking it out of her hand just as she uttered the word "peep".

Green light flew out of the wand, but instead of hitting Tyra and Bethany the light hit two of the other dancers. Dropping their costumes, the dancers yawned and stretched sleepily. Then they both slowly sank to the floor, resting their heads on their arms.

"No!" cried Tyra. "Don't fall asleep!"

But the two dancers were powerless to resist Princess Poison's sleeping spell. They curled up and shut their eyes. A moment later, they were fast asleep, snoring gently.

"Wake up!" Tyra said, shaking one girl's shoulder.

"It's time for the finale!" shouted Bethany. She clapped her hands, trying to wake up the other girl.

It was no use. The dancers were in a deep, enchanted slumber.

"The routine will be ruined without them," wailed Tyra. "The choreography will be all messed up."

"And the lifts won't work," Bethany added.

"Oh dear," sneered Princess Poison. "You snooze, you lose!" Then, with a wave of her wand and a flash of green light, she and Hex vanished.

"Can you help us?" Tyra pleaded.

"I wish we could," said Mia. "But we used our last wish to fix the music."

"You don't need magic," said Bethany. "You and Charlotte can take their places. You learned the routine at the audition and watched us rehearsing it today when you arrived – I'm sure you could do it."

"That's a great idea," said Tyra.

"Oh no," said Mia, shaking her head. "I couldn't. Charlotte's the dancer – not me."

"But we need two dancers," said Bethany.

Charlotte could see that Mia was nervous about performing – she preferred to stay out of the spotlight. But Charlotte knew she had to persuade her – they couldn't let Princess Poison spoil the show.

"You are a good dancer, Mia. You did the routine really well at the auditions. And you won't be alone – I'll be on stage with you."

"So will we," said Bethany.

"I'm not sure …" said Mia.

"Please," begged Tyra. "Pretty, pretty please? With sugar on top?"

"You told us that friendship is more powerful than magic," Bethany reminded her.

Mia looked at Charlotte beseechingly. Charlotte took Mia's hand and gave it an encouraging squeeze.

"OK, I'll do it," said Mia. She smiled bravely, though Charlotte felt her hand trembling with fright. "The show must go on."

"Thank you!" said Tyra, throwing her arms around Mia's neck.

Bethany held up the costumes that belonged to the sleeping dancers. "Let's go!"

Mia and Charlotte quickly wriggled into sparkling pink tights and the poufy tutus. They slipped their feet into the dancers' soft dance shoes. Luckily, everything fit.

"I feel sorry for these two," said Mia, looking down at the dozing dancers.

"Me too," said Charlotte as she tied her hair up in a bun. "At least they got to dance in some of the other routines."

The sound of applause came from the hall as the tap-dancing chocolates finished their routine. The dancers ran into the rehearsal

room, their shoes clattering on the floor.

"You're on!" a dancer in a shiny purple costume told the girls.

"Wish me luck," said Mia as they followed Bethany and Tyra on to the stage.

"You're going to be amazing," Charlotte reassured her. "Just like the whole show."

The band struck up the first notes of Alice's Christmas song. It was time to dance!

The Masked Ball

Charlotte shimmied, sashayed and spun along with the other dancers. It had been weeks since the audition, but she still remembered the moves perfectly. Exhilarated, she leaped high in the air.

Out of the corner of her eye, Charlotte saw Mia smiling as she danced to Alice's song. *It's as if Alice is here, helping us,* thought

Charlotte, smiling to herself.

As the band played the final chorus, Charlotte helped the dancers lift Bethany high into the air. Mia helped lift Tyra up. The Christmas Fairies each balanced on one leg, their wings fluttering and their wands held up high, until the stage curtains swished shut.

There was a moment of silence and then the audience burst into applause!

When the curtains opened again, each group of dancers curtseyed and the audience cheered and leapt up to give them a standing ovation!

Bethany's mum blew her a kiss.

"Bravo!" cheered Tyra's parents, beaming with pride.

Miss Anastasia came onstage, holding two bouquets of roses. Presenting them to Tyra and Bethany, she said, "I'm so proud of you two. The show was wonderful."

Behind her glasses, Bethany's eyes filled with tears of joy. Tyra grinned, her shiny braces sparkling in the spotlight. The two soloists held hands and raised them triumphantly in the air.

Charlotte and Mia grinned at each other.
The girls' second wish had been granted!
Suddenly, snow magically started to fall inside
the hall, drifting down in big white flakes.

"Oooh!" everyone gasped, trying to catch the
snowflakes. Mia and Charlotte grinned. The
snow wasn't a special effect – it was because
they had granted a second wish!

A snowflake landed on Mia's nose and Charlotte brushed it away. "We did it," she said.

"We did," said Mia. "The show was amazing."

Charlotte heard soft clapping coming from the side of the stage. Turning to see who it was, she gasped.

"Alice!" cried Mia.

"The palace is back to normal!" Alice said.

"So the ball can go ahead?" asked Charlotte, remembering Alice and Ella's plan for Christmas Eve. "Won't the other princesses be arriving soon?"

"That's why I've come to get you," said Alice. "I wouldn't want you to miss out on all the fun. There wouldn't even be a ball if it wasn't for you."

"Can we say goodbye to Tyra and Bethany first?" asked Mia.

"Of course," said Alice.

The girls hurried over to the dancers. They were holding their bouquets and smiling as people congratulated them.

Tapping Tyra on the shoulder, Charlotte whispered, "We've got to go."

Tyra beckoned Bethany over and they stepped away from the crowd.

"Thank you for making our wishes come true," said Tyra. "The show was awesome."

"I used to dream of becoming a dancer," said Bethany. "But now I want to be a Secret Princess, too!"

Waving goodbye, Mia and Charlotte returned to Alice. A wave of her wand brought them to the Wishing Star Palace ballroom. The ice and snow had vanished and a fire was crackling in the enormous fireplace. A big red Christmas stocking was hanging from the mantelpiece.

"Just in time!" said a princess in a turquoise ballgown with a billowing skirt. Ella took off her jewelled mask and smiled at them.

"The decorations look beautiful," said Alice, admiring the swags of holly and pine.

"Everything's ready for the ball," said Ella.

"Except for you three." She waved her wand and suddenly Alice was wearing a long purple gown. Mia and Charlotte had ballgowns on, too. Mia's was crimson velvet and Charlotte's was emerald green satin, and they each had a feathered mask to match.

"Let's get this party started!" cried Alice, waving her wand.

Music started to play and a lavish banquet table magically appeared. There was a tower of cream cakes glistening with toffee sauce, white meringues shaped like snowmen and a chocolate log covered in rich swirls of icing. Charlotte's mouth watered in anticipation.

"Happy Christmas!" called a princess in a yellow ballgown as she took off her mask. It was Princess Evie! She was soon joined by Princess Sylvie, Princess Cara and Princess Phoebe. More and more Secret Princesses arrived, all wearing beautiful gowns and masks.

Holding her wand like a microphone, Alice started to sing one of her pop songs.

Mia and Charlotte danced all around the ballroom with their princess friends.

Everyone cheered when Alice launched into her new hit, *Christmas Dream:*

"Christmas is a dream come true,

Because I'm spending it with you!"

Charlotte smiled at Mia as they danced. Alice's lyrics were perfect!

Just before midnight, Ella called everyone over to the window. "Look at the sky!"

Mia and Charlotte gazed up at the Northern Lights. The night sky shimmered with luminous streaks of pink and purple.

"What's that?" asked Charlotte, squinting at something flying overhead. It looked like a sleigh …

"It's Santa!" said Alice. "And it looks like he stopped by to fill up our magic stocking."

She led them over to the fireplace and took down the Christmas stocking that hung over the fireplace. "You two go first."

Charlotte reached into the stocking and felt around for the perfect present. She took out a little box tied with a red ribbon. "It's gorgeous!" she said, opening her gift and taking out a silver key ring shaped like a ballet slipper.

Next, Mia dipped her hand into the stocking and took out another small box. "I got one too!" she squealed, opening the box and holding up her own key ring.

"It's getting late," said Alice. "You should probably head home."

"Aw," said Charlotte. "We're having so much fun."

"You need to get some rest before Christmas," said Alice, smiling. "But you can use your key rings to make a special Christmas wish."

"Happy Christmas," Mia said, hugging Charlotte goodbye.

As the princesses sang carols around the Christmas tree, Alice waved her wand and sent Mia and Charlotte home.

Back in her bedroom, Charlotte held her
ballet key ring to her heart and whispered,
"I wish I could see Mia this Christmas." She
didn't know for sure, but she thought Mia
might make the same wish, just like Tyra and
Bethany had. After all, they were best friends.
She put the key ring away, then changed into
her pyjamas and ran downstairs.

"Before you go to bed," said Charlotte's
mum, "Dad and I wanted to give you all an
early Christmas present." She handed them an
envelope from under the Christmas tree.

Charlotte opened it and found tickets for
a pantomime. "I don't understand," she said,
confused. "How can we go to see *Cinderella*?
It's in England."

Charlotte's parents grinned.

"We're flying there on Boxing Day," her dad explained. "We're going to stay with Nana and Grandad for a week."

"And Mia and her family are coming to the pantomime with us!" said Mum.

"This is going to be the best Christmas ever," Charlotte said, hugging her parents tight. After a sunny Christmas Day in California, she was going to see Mia in England.

Her Christmas wish was coming true!

The End

Join Charlotte and Mia in their next Secret Princesses adventure!

Read on for a sneak peek!

Star Science

"Don't let go!" cried Elsie, Mia Thompson's little sister.

"I won't," panted Mia, holding on to the back of Elsie's pink bike and running to keep up as her sister pedalled. "You're doing great!"

DING! DING!

Elsie rang her bike bell proudly. Their mum looked up from the magazine she was reading on a nearby bench and gave them a thumbs up.

They had been in the park all afternoon,

teaching Elsie how to ride her bike without stabilisers. The sun was beginning to set, but Elsie still hadn't quite got the hang of it yet.

As they reached the end of the path, Elsie squeezed her brakes and the bike squealed to a stop.

"Well done," gasped Mia, clutching her side and trying to catch her breath. Teaching someone how to ride a bike was exhausting!

Elsie turned her bike around. "This time, I want to try all by myself," she said.

"OK," said Mia. "I'll start you off, then I'll let go. Ready?"

Elsie nodded determinedly and gripped the handlebars. As she started to pedal, Mia

jogged along behind her, holding the back
of the seat lightly. When they were halfway
down the path, she let go.

For a few moments, Elsie cycled forward on
her own. But then she glanced back at Mia
for reassurance – and wobbled off to the side.

"Woah!" wailed Elsie.

"Don't look at me," coached Mia. "Watch
where you are going!"

It was too late. Elsie had lost her balance.
The bike wobbled and then—

CRASH!

Elsie flew off the bike and sprawled onto
the path. The bike lay on top of her, its
wheels spinning wildly.

"Are you OK?" cried Mia, running over

to her sister. She lifted the bike off Elsie and helped her sit up. There was blood on Elsie's knee. "Does it hurt?"

Elsie nodded, her bottom lip wobbling.

"You poor thing," said Mia, giving Elsie a big hug.

Mia could tell that her little sister was trying to fight back tears, but one escaped and fell onto Mia's shoulder with a plop.

"I'm never going to learn how to ride a bike," sobbed Elsie.

"Of course you will," Mia said, rubbing her sister's back gently. "It took me ages to learn how to ride a bike, too."

"Really?" asked Elsie, sniffling.

"Yup," confirmed Mia. "Charlotte learned

how to ride without stabilisers way before me. But then, she's good at anything sporty." Charlotte Williams was Mia's best friend in the whole world. The summer Mia had learned how to ride a bike, the two of them had spent hours cycling around the park together. A while back, Charlotte's family had moved to California, but the girls still saw each other – because they shared a magical secret!

"Is my bike OK?" asked Elsie, interrupting Mia's thoughts.

Mia propped the bike against a tree and inspected it for damage. It was decorated with pictures of princesses and had pink and purple tassels dangling from the handlebars.

There was even a white basket with plastic daisies attached to the front.

"It's fine," said Mia.

"Phew," said Elsie. "I'm glad the princesses didn't get scratched." She sighed longingly. "I wish I was a princess. Then I could wear a beautiful tiara instead of a boring old bike helmet."

Mia laughed. "Even princesses wear helmets when they go cycling."

Elsie shook her head emphatically. "No, princesses don't ride bikes. They just dance at fancy balls and wear sparkly tiaras."

Mia thought about the princesses she knew. Though they did like dancing at balls and wearing tiaras, they also did lots of other cool things – like swimming, painting and horse riding. They had jobs too – one was a vet, another was a teacher, and there was even a pop star! Of course she couldn't tell Elsie any of this, because her princess friends were Secret Princesses! They kept the fact that they could grant wishes using magic a secret. They only wore their tiaras when they visited Wishing Star Palace, a magical place hidden in the clouds. The only reason Mia knew any of this was because she and Charlotte were training to become Secret Princess too!

"Let's get you cleaned up," said Mia, helping Elsie to her feet.

As they wheeled the bike back to where

their mum was sitting, Elsie pointed up at the sky. "Look, Mia."

A full moon was peeking out from behind pink clouds as the afternoon turned into twilight.

"It's pretty," said Mia.

"Is the moon really made of cheese?" Elsie asked curiously.

"No," said Mia, with a giggle. "I think it's made of rock."

"What type of rock?" asked Elsie.

"I'm not sure," said Mia. "But we can look it up on the computer when we get home."

Thinking about the moon reminded Mia of the four moonstones she and Charlotte needed to earn for the next stage of their

training. Mia couldn't wait to get started –
it felt like ages since she'd seen Charlotte.
Looking down at the necklace she always
wore, Mia's heart leapt. The half-heart
pendant was glowing!

"Oh dear," Mum said, catching sight of
Elsie's knee as they approached. Rummaging
in her handbag, Mum dug out a tissue and
a plaster. She dabbed away the blood and
stuck the plaster on Elsie's knee.

"There!" she said, smiling. "As good as
new!"

Elsie smiled back bravely.

Tucking her magazine into her handbag,
Mum stood up and said, "It's going to be dark
soon. Why don't we let Mia have a quick

bike ride, and I'll help you, Elsie."

"Thanks, Mum!" Mia said.

She got onto her bike, which was the exact same shade of blue as her eyes. Strapping on her helmet, Mia pedalled off as fast as she could go, her long blonde hair streaming out behind her. When she was sure that she was out of sight, Mia stoppe and rested her bike against a tree.

Ducking behind the tree, Mia grasped her glowing necklace. "I wish I could be with Charlotte," she said.

The light shining out of the pendant grew brighter and brighter. It swirled around Mia, until she was surrounded by a sparkly magical glow. She wasn't worried about leaving her bike behind – no time would pass here while she was having a Secret Princess adventure.

Read Star Science to find out what happens next!

Bethany and Tyra's Beginner Ballet!

The first ballet steps to learn are the five positions.

- First Position: move your feet so your heels touch each other and your toes are pointing out in opposite directions
- Second Position: keep your toes in first position, but place your feet about a foot apart
- Third Position: keeping your toes pointed out, put the heel of one of your feet in the middle of the other one
- Fourth Position: same as third, but put a gap between your feet
- Fifth Position: similar to first, but put the heel of one foot at the toe of the other

Can you do them all?

Ballet Dictionary

Miss Anastasia uses lots of funny
ballet words. Read Tyra and Bethany's
ballet dictionary below and talk like a ballerina!

Arabesque
Stand on one leg with the other leg out with a straight knee

Barre
The barre is a wooden or metal bar that ballerinas lean on while they're practising

Chassé
Step forward with one foot then 'chase' it with the next

Demi
Demi means half, and is used in lots of ballet terms.
Demi-plie means 'half bend at the knees'

Étoile

Étoile means star, and means the leading dancer

Grande

Grande meaning 'big' or 'large'. Grande allegro means big jumps.

Plié

A plié is bending your knees. Pliés can be done in any position

Pirouette

A one-legged spin with the foot of the raised leg touching the other one

Secret PRINCESSES

What would you wish for?

Are you a Secret Princess?

Join the Secret Princesses Club at:

secretprincessesbooks.co.uk

Explore the magic of the
Secret Princesses and discover:

♥ Special competitions! ♥
♥ Exclusive content! ♥
♥ All the latest princess news! ♥